"WONDERFUL . . . PLUNGES US INTO THE STRANGE, MAGICAL, SHIFTING WORLD OF CHILDHOOD IN THE WEST INDIES."
—*Philadelphia Inquirer*

"A treasure: intricate, delicate . . . These 10 stories, usually in the first person present tense, take you, wide-eyed and barefoot, into *places.* . . . Read Kincaid . . . for the wonder and astonishment of being."
—*Charlotte Observer*

"What she knows is rare: pure passion, a past filled with curious events, a voice, humor, and above all a craft. . . . Her language recalls Henri Rousseau's painting: seemingly natural, but in reality sophisticated and precise."
—*The Village Voice*

"Rich, stirring prose and keen vision . . . There are a hundred charms in this collection of short stories."
—*West Coast Review of Books*

"Some [of the stories] talk of the empathy between mothers or fathers and daughters, others of the irreducible differences between men and women, or the power of nature and the mystery in the most ordinary objects. . . . They make the familiar seem strange, the exotic seem commonplace. No one else seems to be writing quite this way right now."
—*Los Angeles Times Book Review*

JAMAICA KINCAID was born in Antigua, of which she remains a citizen. Many of her stories originally appeared in *The New Yorker,* and she is the author of the highly acclaimed books *Annie John, A Small Place,* and *Lucy.* She now lives with her husband, her daughter, and her son in Vermont.

Jamaica Kincaid

AT THE BOTTOM

OF THE RIVER

A PLUME BOOK

PLUME
Published by the Penguin Group
Penguin Books USA Inc., 375 Hudson Street,
New York, New York 10014, U.S.A.
Penguin Books Ltd, 27 Wrights Lane, London W8 5TZ, England
Penguin Books Australia Ltd, Ringwood, Victoria, Australia
Penguin Books Canada Ltd, 10 Alcorn Avenue,
Toronto, Ontario, Canada M4V 3B2
Penguin Books (N.Z.) Ltd, 182-190 Wairau Road, Auckland 10, New Zealand

Penguin Books Ltd, Registered Offices: Harmondsworth, Middlesex, England

Published by Plume, an imprint of New American Library, a division of
Penguin Books USA Inc. Published by arrangement with Farrar, Straus &
Giroux, Inc.

First Plume Printing, January, 1992
10 9 8 7 6 5 4 3 2 1

Acknowledgment is made to *The New Yorker* for the following stories, which first
appeared in its pages: "Girl," "In the Night," "At Last," "Wingless," "Holi-
days," "The Letter from Home," and "At the Bottom of the River," and to *The
Paris Review* for "What I Have Been Doing Lately." The excerpt at the beginning of "Wingless" is from *The Water Babies* by Charles Kingsley.

 REGISTERED TRADEMARK—MARCA REGISTRADA

LIBRARY OF CONGRESS CATALOGING-IN-PUBLICATION DATA
Kincaid, Jamaica.
    At the bottom of the river / Jamaica Kincaid.
      p.   cm.
    Contents: Girl — In the night — At last — Wingless — Holidays —
The letter from home — What I have been doing lately — Blackness —
My mother — At the bottom of the river.
    ISBN 0-452-26754-4
    1. Caribbean Area—Fiction.   I. Title.
PR9275.A583K5635   1992
813—dc20   91-31036
                                                                      CIP

Printed in the United States of America

Original hardcover design by Cynthia Krupat

PUBLISHER'S NOTE
These are works of fiction. Names, characters, places, and incidents either are
the product of the author's imagination or are used fictitiously, and any re-
semblance to actual persons, living or dead, events, or locales is entirely coinci-
dental.

For my mother, Annie, with love, and

for Mr. Shawn, with gratitude and love

Contents

❧

At the Bottom of the River

GIRL

ash the white clothes on Monday and put them on the stone heap; wash the color clothes on Tuesday and put them on the clothesline to dry; don't walk barehead in the hot sun; cook pumpkin fritters in very hot sweet oil; soak your little cloths right after you take them off; when buying cotton to make yourself a nice blouse, be sure that it doesn't have gum on it, because that way it won't hold up well after a wash; soak salt fish overnight before you cook it; is it true that you sing benna in Sunday school?; always eat your food in such a way that it won't turn someone else's stomach; on Sundays try to walk like a lady and not like the slut you are so bent on becoming; don't sing benna in Sunday school; you mustn't speak to wharf-rat boys, not even to give directions; don't eat fruits on the street—flies will follow you; *but I don't sing benna on Sundays at all and never in Sunday school*; this is how to sew on a button; this is how to make a buttonhole for the button you have just sewed on; this is how to hem a dress when you see the hem coming down and so to prevent yourself from looking like the slut I know you are so bent on becoming; this is how you iron your father's khaki shirt so that it doesn't have a crease; this is how you iron your father's khaki pants so that they don't have a crease; this is how you grow okra—far from the house, because okra tree harbors red ants; when you are growing dasheen, make sure it gets plenty of water or else it makes your throat itch when you are eating it; this is how you sweep a corner; this is how you sweep a whole house; this is how you sweep a yard; this is how you smile to someone you don't like too much; this is how you smile to someone you don't like at all; this is how you smile to someone you like completely; this is how you set a table for tea; this is how you set a table for dinner; this is how you set a table for dinner with an important guest; this is how you set a table for lunch; this is how you set a table for breakfast; this is how to behave in the presence of men who don't know you very well, and this way they won't recognize immediately the slut I have warned you against becoming; be sure to wash every day, even if it is with your own spit; don't squat down to play marbles—you are not a boy, you know; don't pick people's flowers—you might catch something; don't throw stones at blackbirds, because it might not be a blackbird at all; this is how to make a bread pudding; this is how to make doukona; this is how to make pepper pot; this is how to make a good medicine for a cold; this is how to make a good medicine to throw away a child before it even becomes a child; this is how to catch a fish; this is how to throw back a fish you don't like, and that way something bad won't fall on you; this is how to bully a man; this is how a man bullies you; this is how to love a man, and if this doesn't work there are other ways, and if they don't work don't feel too bad about giving up; this is how to spit up in the air if you feel like it, and this is how to move quick so that it doesn't fall on you; this is how to make ends meet; always squeeze bread to make sure it's fresh; *but what if the baker won't let me feel the bread?*; you mean to say that after all you are really going to be the kind of woman who the baker won't let near the bread?

IN THE NIGHT

In the night, way into the middle of the night, when the night isn't divided like a sweet drink into little sips, when there is no just before midnight, midnight, or just after midnight, when the night is round in some places, flat in some places, and in some places like a deep hole, blue at the edge, black inside, the night-soil men come.

They come and go, walking on the damp ground in straw shoes. Their feet in the straw shoes make a scratchy sound. They say nothing.

The night-soil men can see a bird walking in trees. It isn't a bird. It is a woman who has removed her skin and is on her way to drink the blood of her secret enemies. It is a woman who has left her skin in a corner of a house made out of wood. It is a woman who is reasonable and admires honeybees in the hibiscus. It is a woman who, as a joke, brays like a donkey when he is thirsty.

There is the sound of a cricket, there is the sound of a church bell, there is the sound of this house creaking, that house creaking, and the other house creaking as they settle into the ground. There is the sound of a radio in the distance—a fisherman listening to merengue music. There is the sound of a man groaning in his sleep; there is the sound of a woman disgusted at the man groaning. There is the sound of the man stabbing the woman, the sound of her blood as it hits the floor, the sound of Mr. Straffee, the undertaker, taking her body away. There is the sound of her spirit back from the dead, looking at the man who used to groan; he is running a fever forever. There is the sound of a woman writing a letter; there is the sound of her pen nib on the white writing paper; there is the sound of the kerosene lamp dimming; there is the sound of her head aching.

The rain falls on the tin roofs, on the leaves in the trees, on the stones in the yard, on sand, on the ground. The night is wet in some places, warm in some places.

There is Mr. Gishard, standing under a cedar tree which is in full bloom, wearing that nice white suit, which is as fresh as the day he was buried in it. The white suit came from England in a brown package: "To: Mr. John Gishard," and so on and so on. Mr.

Gishard is standing under the tree, wearing his nice suit and holding a glass full of rum in his hand—the same glass full of rum that he had in his hand shortly before he died—and looking at the house in which he used to live. The people who now live in the house walk through the door backward when they see Mr. Gishard standing under the tree, wearing his nice white suit. Mr. Gishard misses his accordion; you can tell by the way he keeps tapping his foot.

In my dream I can hear a baby being born. I can see its face, a pointy little face—so nice. I can see its hands—so nice, again. Its eyes are closed. It's breathing, the little baby. It's breathing. It's bleating, the little baby. It's bleating. The baby and I are now walking to pasture. The baby is eating green grass with its soft and pink lips. My mother is shaking me by the shoulders. My mother says, "Little Miss, Little Miss." I say to my mother, "But it's still night." My mother says, "Yes, but you have wet your bed again." And my mother, who is still young, and still beautiful, and still has pink lips, removes my wet nightgown, removes my wet sheets from my bed. My mother can change everything. In my dream I am in the night.

"What are the lights in the mountains?"

"The lights in the mountains? Oh, it's a jablesse."

"A jablesse! But why? What's a jablesse?"

"It's a person who can turn into anything. But you can tell they aren't real because of their eyes. Their eyes shine like lamps, so bright that you can't look. That's how you can tell it's a jablesse. They like to go up in the mountains and gallivant. Take good care when you see a beautiful woman. A jablesse always tries to look like a beautiful woman."

No one has ever said to me, "My father, a night-soil man, is very nice and very kind. When he passes a dog, he gives a pat and not a kick. He likes all the parts of a fish but especially the head. He goes to church quite regularly and is always glad when the minister calls out, 'A Mighty Fortress Is Our God,' his favorite hymn. He would like to wear pink shirts and pink pants but knows that this color isn't very becoming to a man, so instead he wears navy blue and brown, colors he does not like at all. He met my mother on what masquerades as a bus around here, a long time ago, and he still likes to whistle. Once, while running to catch a bus, he fell and broke his ankle and had to spend a week in hospital. This made him miserable, but he cheered up quite a bit when he saw my mother and me, standing over his white cot, holding bunches of yellow roses and smiling down at him. Then he said, 'Oh, my. Oh, my.' What he likes to do most, my father the night-soil man, is to sit on a big stone under a mahogany tree and watch small children playing play-cricket while he eats the intestines of animals stuffed with blood and rice and drinks ginger beer. He has told me this many times: 'My dear, what I like to do most,' and so on. He is always reading botany books and knows a lot about rubber plantations and rubber trees; but this is an interest I can't explain, since the only rubber tree he has ever seen is a specially raised one in the botanic gardens. He sees to it that my school shoes fit comfortably. I love my father the night-soil man. My mother loves my father the night-soil man. Everybody loves him and waves to him whenever they see him. He is very handsome, you know, and I have seen women look at him twice. On special days he wears a brown felt hat, which he orders from England, and brown leather shoes, which he also orders from England. On ordinary days he goes barehead. When he calls me, I say, 'Yes, sir.' On my mother's birthday he always buys her some nice cloth for a new dress as a present. He makes us happy, my father the night-soil man, and has promised that one day he will take us to see something he has read about called the circus."

⤸

In the night, the flowers close up and thicken. The hibiscus flowers, the flamboyant flowers, the bachelor's buttons, the irises, the marigolds, the whitehead-bush flowers, the lilies, the flowers on the daggerbush, the flowers on the turtleberry bush, the flowers on the soursop tree, the flowers on the sugar-apple tree, the flowers on the mango tree, the flowers on the guava tree, the flowers on the cedar tree, the flowers on the stinking-toe tree, the flowers on the dumps tree, the flowers on the papaw tree, the flowers everywhere close up and thicken. The flowers are vexed.

Someone is making a basket, someone is making a girl a dress or a boy a shirt, someone is making her husband a soup with cassava so that he can take it to the cane field tomorrow, someone is making his wife a beautiful mahogany chest, someone is sprinkling a colorless powder outside a closed door so that someone else's child will be stillborn, someone is praying that a bad child who is living prosperously abroad will be good and send a package filled with new clothes, someone is sleeping.

Now I am a girl, but one day I will marry a woman—a red-skin woman with black bramblebush hair and brown eyes, who wears skirts that are so big I can easily bury my head in them. I would like to marry this woman and live with her in a mud hut near the sea. In the mud hut will be two chairs and one table, a lamp that burns kerosene, a medicine chest, a pot, one bed, two pillows, two sheets, one looking glass, two cups, two saucers, two dinner plates, two forks, two drinking-water glasses, one china pot, two fishing strings, two straw hats to ward the hot sun off our heads, two trunks for things we have very little use for, one basket, one book of plain paper, one box filled with twelve crayons of different colors, one loaf of bread wrapped in a piece of brown paper, one coal pot, one picture of two women standing on a jetty, one picture of the same two women embracing, one picture of the same two women waving goodbye, one box of matches. Every day this red-skin woman and I will eat bread and milk for breakfast, hide in bushes and throw hardened cow dung at people we don't like, climb coconut trees, pick coconuts, eat and drink the food and water from the coconuts we have picked, throw stones in the sea, put on John Bull masks and frighten defenseless little children on their way home from school, go fishing and catch only our favorite fishes to roast and have for dinner, steal green figs to eat for dinner with the roast fish. Every day we would do this. Every night I would sing this woman a song; the words I don't know yet, but the tune is in my head. This woman I would like to marry knows many things, but to me she will only tell about things that would never dream of making me cry; and every night, over and over, she will tell me something that begins, "Before you were born." I will marry a woman like this, and every night, every night, I will be completely happy.

AT LAST

THE HOUSE

F lived in this house with you: the wood shingles, unpainted, weather-beaten, fraying; the piano, a piece of furniture now, collecting dust; the bed in which all the children were born; a bowl of flowers, alive, then dead; a bowl of fruit, but then all eaten. (What was that light?) My hair-brush is full of dead hair. Where are the letters that brought the bad news? Where are they? These glasses commemorate a coronation. What are you now? A young woman. But what are you really? A young woman. I know how hard that is. If only everything would talk. The floorboards made a nice pattern when the sun came in. (Was that the light again?) At night, after cleaning the soot from the lampshade, I lighted the lamp and, before preparing

for bed, planned another day. So many things I
forgot, though. I hid something under the bed, but
then I forgot, and it spawned a feathery white moss,
so beautiful; it stank, and that's how I remembered
it was there. Now I am looking at you; your lips are
soft and parted.

Are they?

I saw the cat open its jaws wide and I saw the
roof of its mouth, which was pink with black shad-
ing, and its teeth looked white and sharp and dangerous. I had no shells from the sea, which was minutes
away. This beautifully carved shelf: you can touch
it now. Why did I not let you eat with your bare
hands when you wanted to?

Why were all the doors closed so tight shut?

But they weren't closed.

I saw them closed.

What passed between us then? You asked me if
it was always the way it is now. But I don't know.
I wasn't always here. I wasn't here in the beginning.
We held hands once and were beautiful. But what
followed? Sleepless nights, oh, sleepless nights. A
baby was born on Thursday and was almost eaten,
eyes first, by red ants, on Friday. (But the light,
where does it come from, the light?) I've walked
the length of this room so many times, by now I
have traveled a desert.

With me?

With you. Speak in a whisper. I like the way your lips purse when you whisper. You are a woman. Stand over there near the dead flowers. I can see your reflection in the glass bowl. You are soft and curved like an arch. Your limbs are large and un-knotted, your feet unsnared. (It's the light again, now in flashes.)

Was it like a carcass? Did you feed on it?

Yes.

Or was it like a skeleton? Did you live in it?

Yes, that too. We prayed. But what did we pray for? We prayed to be saved. We prayed to be blessed. We prayed for long and happy lives for our children. And always we prayed to see the morning light. Were we saved? I don't know. To this day I don't know. We filled the rooms; I filled the rooms. Eggs boiled violently in that pot. When the hurri-cane came, we hid in this corner until the wind passed; the rain that time, the rain that time. The foundation of this house shook and the earth washed away. My skin grew hot and damp; then I shivered with excitement.

What did you say to me? What did I not hear?

The mattress was stuffed with coconut fiber. It was our first mattress. It made our skin raw. It harbored bedbugs. I used to stand here, at this window, look-ing out at the shadows of people passing—and they were real people—and I would run my hand over the pattern of ridges in the cover belonging to the kettle. I used to stand over here too, in front of this mirror, and I would run my hands across the stitches in a new tablecloth. And again I would stand here, in front of the cold stove, and run my fingers through a small bag of green coffee beans. In this cage lived a hummingbird. He died after a few days, homesick for the jungle. I tried to take everything one day at a time, just as it was coming up.

And then?

I felt sick. Always I felt sick. I sat in this rocking chair with you on my lap. Let me calm her, I thought, let me calm her. But in my breast my milk soured.

So I was loved?

Yes. You wore your clothes wrapped tight around your body, keeping your warmth to yourself. What greed! But how could you know? A yellow liquid left a stain here.

Is that blood?

Yes, but who bled? That picture of an asphalt lake. He visited an asphalt lake once. He loved me then. I was beautiful. I built a fire. The coals glowed so. Bitter. Bitter. Bitter. There was music, there was dancing. Again and again we touched, and again and again we were beautiful. I could see that. I could see some things. I cried. I could not see everything. What illness was it that caused the worm to crawl out of his leg the day he died? Someone laughed

here. I heard that, and just then I was made happy.
Look. You were dry and warm and solid and small.
I was soft and curved like an arch. I wore blue, bird
blue, and at night I would shine in the dark.

The children?

They weren't here yet, the children. I could hear
their hearts beating, but they weren't here yet. They
were beautiful, but not the way you are. Sometimes
I appeared as a man. Sometimes I appeared as a
hoofed animal, stroking my own brown, shiny back.
Then I left no corner unturned. Nothing frightened
me. A blind bird dashed its head against this closed
window. I heard that. I crossed the open sea alone
at night on a steamer. What was my name—I mean
the name my mother gave to me—and where did I
come from? My skin is now coarse. What pity. What
sorrow. I have made a list. I have measured everything. I have not lied.

But the light. What of the light?

Splintered. Died.

THE YARD

A mountain. A valley. The shade. The sun.

A streak of yellow rapidly conquering a streak of
green. Blending and separating. Children are so
quick: quick to laugh, quick to brand, quick to scorn,
quick to lay claim to the open space.

The thud of small feet running, running. A girl's

shriek—snaps in two. Tumbling, tumbling, the sound of a noon bell. Dry? Wet? Warm? Cold? Nothing is measured here.

An old treasure rudely broken. See how the amber color fades from its rim. Now it is the home of something dark and moist. An ant walking on a sheet of tin laid bare to the sun—crumbles. But what is an ant? Secreting, secreting; always secreting. The skin of an orange—removed as if it had been a decorous and much-valued belt. A frog, beaded and creased, moldy and throbbing—no more than a single leap in a single day.

(But at last, at last, to whom will this view belong? Will the hen, stripped of its flesh, its feathers scattered perhaps to the four corners of the earth, its bones molten and sterilized, one day speak? And what will it say? I was a hen? I had twelve chicks? One of my chicks, named Beryl, took a fall?)

Many secrets are alive here. A sharp blow delivered quicker than an eye blink. A sparrow's eggs. A pirate's trunk. A fisherman's catch. A tree, bearing fruits. A bullying boy's marbles. All that used to be is alive here.

Someone has piled up stones, making a small enclosure for a child's garden, and planted a child's flowers, bluebells. Yes, but a child is too quick, and the bluebells fall to the cool earth, dying and living in perpetuity.

Unusually large berries, red, gold, and indigo, sliced open and embedded in soft mud. The duck's bill, hard and sharp and shiny; the duck itself, driven and ruthless. The heat, in waves, coiling and uncoiling until everything seeks shelter in the shade.

Sensing the danger, the spotted beetle pauses, then retraces its primitive crawl. Red fluid rock was deposited here, and now the soil is rich in minerals. On the vines, the ripening vegetables.

But what is a beetle? What is one fly? What is one day? What is anything after it is dead and gone? Another beetle will pause, sensing the danger. Another day, identical to this day . . . then the rain, beating the underbrush hard, causing the turtle to bury its head even more carefully. The stillness comes and the stillness goes. The sun. The moon.

Still the sounds of voices, muted and then clear, emptying and filling up, saying:

"What was the song they used to sing and made fists and pretended to be Romans?"

WINGLESS

The small children are reading from a book filled with simple words and sentences.

" 'Once upon a time there was a little chimney-sweep, whose name was Tom.' "

" 'He cried half his time, and laughed the other half.' "

" 'You would have been giddy, perhaps, at looking down: but Tom was not.' "

" 'You, of course, would have been very cold sitting there on a September night, without the least bit of clothes on your wet back; but Tom was a water-baby, and therefore felt cold no more than a fish.' "

The children have already learned to write their names in beautiful penmanship. They have already learned how many farthings make a penny, how many pennies make a shilling, how many shillings make a pound, how many days in April, how many stone in a ton. Now they singsong here and tumble there, tearing skirts with swift movements. Must Dulcie really cry after thirteen of her play chums have sat on her? There, Dulcie, there. I myself have been kissed by many rude boys with small, damp lips, on their way to boys' drill. I myself have humped girls under my mother's house. But I swim in a shaft of light, upside down, and I can see myself clearly, through and through, from every angle. Perhaps I stand on the brink of a great discovery, and perhaps after I have made my great discovery I will be sent home in chains. Then again, perhaps my life is as predictable as an insect's and I am in my pupa stage. How low can I sink, then? That woman over there, that large-bottomed woman, is important to me. It's for her that I save up my sixpences instead of spending for sweets. Is this a love like no other? And what pain have I caused her? And does she love me? My needs are great, I can see. But there are the children again (of which I am one), shrieking, whether in pain or pleasure I cannot tell. The children, who are beautiful in groupings of three, and who only last night pleaded with their mothers to sing softly to them, are today maiming each other. The children at the end of the day have sour necks, frayed hair, dirt under their fingernails, scuffed shoes, torn clothing. And why? First they must be children.

I shall grow up to be a tall, graceful, and altogether beautiful woman, and I shall impose on large numbers of people my will and also, for my own amusement, great pain. But now. I shall try to see clearly. I shall try to tell differences. I shall try to distinguish the subtle gradations of color in fine cloth, of fingernail length, of manners. That woman over there. Is she cruel? Does she love me? And if not, can I make her? I am not yet tall, beautiful, graceful, and able to impose my will. Now I swim in a shaft of light and can see myself clearly. The schoolhouse is yellow and stands among big green-leaved trees. Inside are our desks and a woman who wears spectacles, playing the piano. Is a girl who can sing "Gaily the troubadour plucked his guitar" in a pleasing way worthy of being my best friend? There is the same girl, unwashed and glistening, setting traps for talking birds. Is she to be one of my temptations? Oh, this must be a love like no other. But how can my limbs that hate be the same limbs that love? How can the same limbs that make me blind make me see? I am defenseless and small. I shall try to see clearly. I shall try to separate and divide things as if they were sums, as if they were drygoods on the grocer's shelves. Is this my mother? Is she here to embarrass me? What shall I say about her behind her back, when she isn't there, long after she has gone? In her smile lies her goodness. Will I always remember that? Am I horrid? And if so, will I always be that way? Not getting my own way causes me to fret so, I clench my fist. My charm is limited, and I haven't learned to smile yet. I have picked many flowers and then deliberately torn them to shreds, petal by petal. I am so unhappy, my face is so wet, and still I can stand up and walk and tell lies in the face of terrible punishments. I can see the great danger in what I am—a defenseless and pitiful child. Here is a list of what I must do. So is my life to be like an apprenticeship in dressmaking, a thorny path to carefully follow or avoid? Inside, standing around the spectacled woman playing the piano, the children are singing a song in harmony. The children's voices: pinks, blues, yellows, violets, all suspended. All is soft, all is embracing, all is comforting. And yet I myself, at my age, have suffered so. My tears, big, have run down my cheeks in uneven lines—my tears, big, and my hands too small to hold them. My tears have been the result of my disappointments. My disappointments stand up and grow ever taller. They will not be lost to me. There they are. Let me pin tags on them. Let me have them registered, like newly domesticated animals. Let me cherish my disappointments, fold them up, tuck them away, close to my breast, because they are so important to me.

But again I swim in a shaft of light, upside down, and I can see myself clearly, through and through, from every angle. Over there, I stand on the brink of a great discovery, and it is possible that like an ancient piece of history my presence will leave room for theories. But who will say? For days my body has been collecting water, but still I won't cry. What is that to me? I am not yet a woman with a terrible and unwanted burden. I am not yet a dog with a cruel and unloving master. I am not yet a tree growing on barren and bitter land. I am not yet the shape of darkness in a dungeon.

Where? What? Why? How then? Oh, that! I am primitive and wingless.

❧

"Don't eat the strings on bananas—they will wrap around your heart and kill you."

"Oh. Is that true?"

"No."

"Is that something to tell children?"

"No. But it's so funny. You should see how you look trying to remove all the strings from the bananas with your monkey fingernails. Frightened?"

"Frightened. Very frightened."

❧

Today, keeping a safe distance, I followed the woman I love when she walked on a carpet of pond lilies. As she walked, she ate some black nuts, pond-lily black nuts. She walked for a long time, saying what must be wonderful things to herself. Then in the middle of the pond she stopped, because a man had stood up suddenly in front of her. I could see that he wore clothes made of tree bark and sticks in his ears. He said things to her and I couldn't make them out, but he said them to her so forcefully that drops of brown water sprang from his mouth. The woman I love put her hands over her ears, shielding herself from the things he said. Then he put wind in his cheeks and blew himself up until in the bright sun he looked like a boil, and the woman I love put her hands over her eyes, shielding herself from the way he looked. Then, instead of removing her cutlass from the folds of her big and beautiful skirt and cutting the man in two at the waist, she only smiled —a red, red smile—and like a fly he dropped dead.

❧

The sea, the shimmering pink-colored sand, the swimmers with hats, two people walking arm in arm, talking in each other's face, dots of water landing on noses, the sea spray on ankles, on over-developed calves, the blue, the green, the black, so deep, so smooth, a great and swift undercurrent,

glassy, the white wavelets, a storm so blinding that
the salt got in our eyes, the sea turning inside out,
shaking everything up like a bottle with sediment, a
boat with two people heaving a brown package
overboard, the mystery, the sharp teeth of that
yellow spotted eel, the wriggle, the smooth lines,
open mouths, families of great noisy birds, families
of great noisy people, families of biting flies, the
sea, following me home, snapping at my heels, all
the way to the door, the sea, the woman.

"I have frightened you? Again, you are frightened of me?"

"You have frightened me. I am very frightened
of you."

"Oh, you should see your face. I wish you could
see your face. How you make me laugh."

And what are my fears? What large cows! When
I see them coming, shall I run and hide face down in
the gutter? Are they really cows? Can I stand in
a field of tall grass and see nothing for miles and
miles? On the other hand, the sky, which is big and
blue as always, has its limits. This afternoon the
wind is loud as in a hurricane. There isn't enough
light. There is a noise—I can't tell where it is coming from. A big box has stamped on it "Handle
Carefully." I have been in a big white building with

curving corridors. I have passed a dead person. There is the woman I love, who is so much bigger than me.

◆◆

That mosquito . . . now a stain on the wall. That lizard, running up and down, up and down . . . now so still. That ant, bloated and sluggish, a purseful of eggs in its jaws . . . now so still. That blue-and-green bird, head held aloft, singing . . . now so still. That land crab, moving slowly, softly, even beautifully, sideways . . . but now so still. That cricket, standing on a tree stem, so ugly, so revolting, I am made so unhappy . . . now so still. That mongoose, now asleep in its hole, now stealing the sleeping chickens, moving so quickly, its eyes like two grains of light . . . now so still. That fly, moving so contentedly from tea bun to tea bun . . . now so still. That butterfly, moving contentedly from beautiful plant to beautiful plant in the early-morning sun . . . now so still. That tadpole, swimming playfully in the shallow water . . . now so still.

I shall cast a shadow and I shall remain unaware.

My hands, brown on this side, pink on this side, now indiscriminately dangerous, now vagabond and prodigal, now cruel and careless, now without remorse or forgiveness, but now innocently slipping into a dress with braided sleeves, now holding an ice-cream cone, now reaching up with longing, now clasped in prayer, now feeling for reassurance, now pleading my desires, now pleasing, and now, even now, so still in bed, in sleep.

HOLIDAYS

I sit on the porch facing the mountains. I sit on a wicker couch looking out the window at a field of day lilies. I walk into a room where someone—an artist, maybe—has stored some empty canvases. I drink a glass of water. I put the empty glass, from which I have just drunk the water, on a table. I notice two flies, one sitting on top of the other, flying around the room. I scratch my scalp, I scratch my thighs. I lift my arms up and stretch them above my head. I sigh. I spin on my heels once. I walk around the dining-room table three times. I see a book lying on the dining-room table, and I pick it up. The book is called *An Illustrated Encyclopedia of Butterflies and Moths*. I leaf through the book, looking only at the pictures, which are bright and beautiful. From my looking through the book, the word "thorax" sticks in my mind. "Thorax," I say, "thorax, thorax," I don't know how many times. I bend over and touch my toes. I stay in that position until I count to one hundred. As I count, I pretend to be counting off balls on a ball frame. As I count the balls, I pretend that they are the colors red, green, blue, and yellow. I walk over to the fireplace. Standing in front of the fireplace, I try to write my name in the dead ashes with my big toe. I cannot write my name in the dead ashes with my big toe. My big toe, now dirty, I try to clean by rubbing it vigorously on a clean royal-blue rug. The royal-blue rug now has a dark spot, and my big toe has a strong burning sensation. Oh, sensation. I am filled with sensation. I feel—oh, how I feel. I feel, I feel, I feel. I have no words right now for how I feel. I take a walk down the road in my bare feet. I feel the stones on the road, hard and sharp against my soft, almost pink soles. Also, I feel the hot sun beating down on my bare neck. It is midday. Did I say that? Must I say that? Oh me, oh my. The road on which I walk barefoot leads to the store—the village store. Should I go to the village store or should I not go to the village store? I can if I want. If I go to the village store, I can buy a peach. The peach will be warm from sitting in a box in the sun. The peach will not taste sweet and the peach will not taste sour. I will know that I am eating a peach only by looking

at it. I will not go to the store. I will sit on the porch
facing the mountains.

I sit on the porch facing the mountains. The porch
is airy and spacious. I am the only person sitting on
the porch. I look at myself. I can see myself. That is,
I can see my chest, my abdomen, my legs, and my
arms. I cannot see my hair, my ears, my face, or my
collarbone. I can feel them, though. My nose is moist
with sweat. Locking my fingers, I put my hands on
my head. I see a bee, a large bumblebee, flying
around aimlessly. I remove my hands from resting
on my head, because my arms are tired. But also I
have just remembered a superstition: if you sit with
your hands on your head, you will kill your mother.
I have many superstitions. I believe all of them.
Should I read a book? Should I make myself something to drink? But what? And hot or cold? Should
I write a letter? I should write a letter. I will
write a letter. "Dear So-and-So, I am . . . and then I
got the brilliant idea . . . I was very amusing . . . I
had enough, I said . . . I saw what I came to see, I
thought . . . I am laughing all the way to the poor-
house. I grinned . . . I just don't know anymore. I
remain, etc." I like my letter. Perhaps I shall keep
my letter to myself. I fold up the letter I have just
written and put it between the pages of the book I
am trying to read. The book is lying in my lap. I look
around me, trying to find something on which to

focus my eyes. I see ten ants. I count them as they wrestle with a speck of food. I am not fascinated by that. I see my toes moving up and down as if they were tapping out a beat. Why are my toes tapping? I am fascinated by that. A song is going through my mind. It goes, "There was a man from British Guiana, Who used to play a piana. His foot slipped, His trousers ripped . . ." I see, I see. Yes. Now. Suddenly I am tired. I am yawning. Perhaps I will take a nap. Perhaps I will take a long nap. Perhaps I will take a nice long nap. Perhaps, while taking my nap, I will have a dream, a dream in which I am not sitting on the porch facing the mountains.

❦

"I have the most sensible small suitcase in New York.

"I have the most sensible small car in New York.

"I will put my sensible small suitcase in my sensible small car and drive on a sensible and scenic road to the country.

"In the country, I live in a sensible house.

"I am a sensible man.

"It is summer.

"Look at that sunset. Too orange.

"These pebbles. Not pebbly enough.

"A house with interesting angles.

"For dinner I will eat scallops. I love the taste of scallops.

"These are my chums—the two boys and the girl. My chums are the most beautiful chums. The two boys know lumberjacks in Canada, and the girl is fragile. After dinner, my chums and I will play cards, and while playing cards we will tell each other jokes —such funny jokes—but later, thinking back, we will be so pained, so unsettled."

The deerflies, stinging and nesting in wet, matted hair; broken bottles at the bottom of the swimming hole; mosquitoes; a family of skunks eating the family garbage; a family of skunks spraying the family dog; washing the family dog with cans of tomato juice to remove the smell of the skunks; a not-too-fast-moving woodchuck crossing the road; running over the not-too-fast-moving woodchuck; the camera forgotten, exposed in the hot sun; the prism in the camera broken, because the camera has been forgotten, exposed in the hot sun; spraining a finger while trying to catch a cricket ball; spraining a finger while trying to catch a softball; stepping on dry brambles while walking on the newly cut hayfields; the hem of a skirt caught in a barbed-wire fence; the great sunstroke, the great pain, the not at all great day spent in bed.

Inside, the house is still. Outside, the blind man takes a walk. It is midday, and the blind man casts a short, fat shadow as he takes a walk. The blind man is a young man, twenty-seven. The blind man has been blind for only ten years. The blind man was infatuated with the driver of his school bus, a woman. No. The blind man was in love with the driver of his school bus, a woman. The blind man saw the driver of his school bus, a woman, kissing a man. The blind man killed the driver of his school bus, a woman, and then tried to kill himself. He did not die, so now he is just a blind man. The blind man is pale and sickly-looking. He doesn't return a greeting. Everybody knows this, and they stay away from him. Not even the dog pays any attention to his comings and goings.

"But things are so funny here."

"But where? But how?"

"We are going to the May fair, but it's July. They are dancing a May dance around a Maypole, but it's July. They are crowning a May queen, but it's July. At Christmas, just before our big dinner, we take a long swim in the warm seawater. After that, we do not bathe, and in the heat the salt dries on our bodies in little rings."

"Aren't things funny here?"

"Yes, things are funny here."

The two boys are fishing in Michigan, catching fish with live frogs. The two boys do not need a comfortable bed and a nice pillow at night, or newly baked bread for breakfast, or roasted beef on Sundays, or hymns in a cathedral, or small-ankled children wearing white caps, or boxes of fruit from the tropics, or nice greetings and sad partings, or light bulbs, or the tremor of fast motor vehicles, or key chains, or a run-down phonograph, or rubbish baskets, or meek and self-sacrificing women, or inkwells, or shaving kits. The two boys have visited the Mark Twain museum in Missouri and taken photographs. The two boys have done many things and taken photographs. Here are the two boys milking two cows in Wyoming. Here are the two boys seated on the hood of their car just after changing the tire. Here are the two boys dressed up as gentlemen. Here are the two boys dressed up as gentlemen and looking for large-breasted women.

That man, a handsome man; that woman, a beautiful woman; those children, such gay children; great laughter; wild and sour berries; wild and sweet berries; pink and blue-black berries; fields with purple flowers, blue flowers, yellow flowers; a long road; a long and curved road; a car with a collapsible top; big laughs; big laughing in the bushes;

no, not the bushes—the barn; no, not the barn—the house; no, not the house—the trees; no, not the trees, no; big laughing all the same; a crushed straw hat that now fits lopsided; milk from a farm; eggs from a farm; a farm; in the mountains, no clear reception on the radio; no radio; no clothes; no free-floating anxiety; no anxiety; no automatic-lighting stoves; a walk to the store; a walk; from afar, the sound of great laughing; the piano; from afar, someone playing the piano; late-morning sleepiness; many, many brown birds; a big blue-breasted bird; a smaller red-breasted bird; food roasted on sticks; ducks; wild ducks; a pond; so many wide smiles; no high heels; buying many funny postcards; sending many funny postcards; taking the rapids; and still, great laughter.

THE LETTER

FROM HOME

milked the cows, I churned the butter, I
stored the cheese, I baked the bread, I brewed
the tea, I washed the clothes, I dressed the children;
the cat meowed, the dog barked, the horse neighed,
the mouse squeaked, the fly buzzed, the goldfish
living in a bowl stretched its jaws; the door banged
shut, the stairs creaked, the fridge hummed, the
curtains billowed up, the pot boiled, the gas hissed
through the stove, the tree branches heavy with snow
crashed against the roof; my heart beat loudly *thud!
thud!*, tiny beads of water gathered on my nose, my
hair went limp, my waist grew folds, I shed my skin;
lips have trembled, tears have flowed, cheeks have
puffed, stomachs have twisted with pain; I went to
the country, the car broke down, I walked back; the
boat sailed, the waves broke, the horizon tipped,

the jetty grew small, the air stung, some heads bobbed, some handkerchiefs fluttered; the drawers didn't close, the faucets dripped, the paint peeled, the walls cracked, the books tilted over, the rug no longer lay out flat; I ate my food, I chewed each mouthful thirty-two times, I swallowed carefully, my toe healed; there was a night, it was dark, there was a moon, it was full, there was a bed, it held sleep; there was movement, it was quick, there was a being, it stood still, there was a space, it was full, then there was nothing; a man came to the door and asked, "Are the children ready yet? Will they bear their mother's name? I suppose you have forgotten that my birthday falls on Monday after next? Will you come to visit me in hospital?"; I stood up, I sat down, I stood up again; the clock slowed down, the post came late, the afternoon turned cool; the cat licked his coat, tore the chair to shreds, slept in a drawer that didn't close; I entered a room, I felt my skin shiver, then dissolve, I lighted a candle, I saw something move, I recognized the shadow to be my own hand, I felt myself to be one thing; the wind was hard, the house swayed, the angiosperms prospered, the mammal-like reptiles vanished (Is the Heaven to be above? Is the Hell below? Does the Lamb still lie meek? Does the Lion roar? Will the streams all run clear? Will we kiss each other deeply later?); in the peninsula some ancient ships are still anchored, in the field the ox stands still, in the village the leopard stalks its prey; the buildings are to be tall, the structures are to be sound, the stairs are to be winding, in the rooms sometimes there is to be a glow; the hats remain on the hat stand, the coats hang dead from the pegs, the hyacinths look as if they will bloom—I know their fragrance will be overpowering; the earth spins on its axis, the axis is imaginary, the valleys correspond to the mountains, the mountains correspond to the sea, the sea corresponds to the dry land, the dry land corresponds to the snake whose limbs are now reduced; I saw a man, He was in a shroud, I sat in a rowboat, He whistled sweetly to me, I narrowed my eyes, He beckoned to me, Come now; I turned and rowed away, as if I didn't know what I was doing.

WHAT I

HAVE BEEN

DOING LATELY

What I have been doing lately: I was lying in bed and the doorbell rang. I ran downstairs. Quick. I opened the door. There was no one there. I stepped outside. Either it was drizzling or there was a lot of dust in the air and the dust was damp. I stuck out my tongue and the drizzle or the damp dust tasted like government school ink. I looked north. I looked south. I decided to start walking north. While walking north, I noticed that I was barefoot. While walking north, I looked up and saw the planet Venus. I said, "It must be almost morning." I saw a monkey in a tree. The tree had no

leaves. I said, "Ah, a monkey. Just look at that.
A monkey." I walked for I don't know how long
before I came up to a big body of water. I wanted to
get across it but I couldn't swim. I wanted to get
across it but it would take me years to build a boat.
I wanted to get across it but it would take me I didn't
know how long to build a bridge. Years passed and
then one day, feeling like it, I got into my boat and
rowed across. When I got to the other side, it was
noon and my shadow was small and fell beneath
me. I set out on a path that stretched out straight
ahead. I passed a house, and a dog was sitting on
the verandah but it looked the other way when it
saw me coming. I passed a boy tossing a ball in the
air but the boy looked the other way when he saw
me coming. I walked and I walked but I couldn't tell
if I walked a long time because my feet didn't feel
as if they would drop off. I turned around to see
what I had left behind me but nothing was familiar.
Instead of the straight path, I saw hills. Instead of
the boy with his ball, I saw tall flowering trees. I
looked up and the sky was without clouds and seemed
near, as if it were the ceiling in my house and, if I
stood on a chair, I could touch it with the tips of my
fingers. I turned around and looked ahead of me
again. A deep hole had opened up before me. I
looked in. The hole was deep and dark and I
couldn't see the bottom. I thought, What's down

there?, so on purpose I fell in. I fell and I fell, over and over, as if I were an old suitcase. On the sides of the deep hole I could see things written, but perhaps it was in a foreign language because I couldn't read them. Still I fell, for I don't know how long. As I fell I began to see that I didn't like the way falling made me feel. Falling made me feel sick and I missed all the people I had loved. I said, I don't want to fall anymore, and I reversed myself. I was standing again on the edge of the deep hole. I looked at the deep hole and I said, You can close up now, and it did. I walked some more without knowing distance. I only knew that I passed through days and nights, I only knew that I passed through rain and shine, light and darkness. I was never thirsty and I felt no pain. Looking at the horizon, I made a joke for myself: I said, "The earth has thin lips," and I laughed.

Looking at the horizon again, I saw a lone figure coming toward me, but I wasn't frightened because I was sure it was my mother. As I got closer to the figure, I could see that it wasn't my mother, but still I wasn't frightened because I could see that it was a woman.

When this woman got closer to me, she looked at me hard and then she threw up her hands. She must have seen me somewhere before because she said,

"It's you. Just look at that. It's you. And just what have you been doing lately?"

I could have said, "I have been praying not to grow any taller."

I could have said, "I have been listening carefully to my mother's words, so as to make a good imitation of a dutiful daughter."

I could have said, "A pack of dogs, tired from chasing each other all over town, slept in the moonlight."

Instead, I said, What I have been doing lately: I was lying in bed on my back, my hands drawn up, my fingers interlaced lightly at the nape of my neck. Someone rang the doorbell. I went downstairs and opened the door but there was no one there. I stepped outside. Either it was drizzling or there was a lot of dust in the air and the dust was damp. I stuck out my tongue and the drizzle or the damp dust tasted like government school ink. I looked north and I looked south. I started walking north. While walking north, I wanted to move fast, so I removed the shoes from my feet. While walking north, I looked up and saw the planet Venus and I said, "If the sun went out, it would be eight minutes before I would know it." I saw a monkey sitting in a tree that had no leaves and I said, "A monkey. Just look at that. A monkey." I picked up a stone and

I threw it at the monkey. The monkey, seeing the stone, quickly moved out of its way. Three times I threw a stone at the monkey and three times it moved away. The fourth time I threw the stone, the monkey caught it and threw it back at me. The stone struck me on my forehead over my right eye, making a deep gash. The gash healed immediately but now the skin on my forehead felt false to me. I walked for I don't know how long before I came to a big body of water. I wanted to get across, so when the boat came I paid my fare. When I got to the other side, I saw a lot of people sitting on the beach and they were having a picnic. They were the most beautiful people I had ever seen. Everything about them was black and shiny. Their skin was black and shiny. Their shoes were black and shiny. Their hair was black and shiny. The clothes they wore were black and shiny. I could hear them laughing and chatting and I said, I would like to be with these people, so I started to walk toward them, but when I got up close to them I saw that they weren't at a picnic and they weren't beautiful and they weren't chatting and laughing. All around me was black mud and the people all looked as if they had been made up out of the black mud. I looked up and saw that the sky seemed far away and nothing I could stand on would make me able to touch it with my fingertips. I thought, If only I could get out of this, so I started to walk. I must have walked for a long time because my feet hurt and felt as if they would drop off. I thought, If only just around the bend I would see my house and inside my house I would find my bed, freshly made at that, and in the kitchen I would find my mother or anyone else that I loved making me a custard. I thought, If only it was a Sunday and I was sitting in a church and I had just heard someone sing a psalm. I felt very sad so I sat down. I felt so sad that I rested my head on my own knees and smoothed my own head. I felt so sad I couldn't imagine feeling any other way again. I said, I don't like this. I don't want to do this anymore. And I went back to lying in bed, just before the doorbell rang.

BLACKNESS

How soft is the blackness as it falls. It falls in silence and yet it is deafening, for no other sound except the blackness falling can be heard. The blackness falls like soot from a lamp with an untrimmed wick. The blackness is visible and yet it is invisible, for I see that I cannot see it. The blackness fills up a small room, a large field, an island, my own being. The blackness cannot bring me joy but often I am made glad in it. The blackness cannot be separated from me but often I can stand outside it. The blackness is not the air, though I breathe it. The blackness is not the earth, though I walk on it. The blackness is not water or food, though I drink and eat it. The blackness is not my blood, though it flows through my veins. The blackness enters my many-tiered spaces and soon the significant word and event recede and eventually vanish: in this way I am annihilated and my form becomes formless and I am absorbed into a vastness of free-flowing matter. In the blackness, then, I have been erased. I can no longer say my own name. I can no longer point to myself and say "I." In the blackness my voice is silent. First, then, I have been my individual self, carefully banishing randomness from my existence, then I am swallowed up in the blackness so that I am one with it ...

There are the small flashes of joy that are present in my daily life: the upturned face to the open sky, the red ball tumbling from small hand to small hand, as small voices muffle laughter; the sliver of orange on the horizon, a remnant of the sun setting. There is the wide stillness, trembling and waiting to be violently shattered by impatient demands.

("May I now have my bread without the crust?"

"But I long ago stopped liking my bread without the crust!")

All manner of feelings are locked up within my human breast and all manner of events summon them out. How frightened I became once on looking down to see an oddly shaped, ash-colored object that I did not recognize at once to be a small part of my own foot. And how powerful I then found that moment, so that I was not at one with myself and I felt myself separate, like a brittle substance dashed and shattered, each separate part without knowledge of the other separate parts. I then clung fast to a common and familiar object (my lamp, as it stood unlit on the clean surface of my mantelpiece), until I felt myself steadied, no longer alone at sea in a small rowboat, the waves cruel and unruly. What is my nature, then? For in isolation I am all purpose and industry and determination and prudence, as if I were the single survivor of a species whose evolutionary history can be traced to the most ancient of ancients; in isolation I ruthlessly plow the deep silences, seeking my opportunities like a miner seeking veins of treasure. In what shallow glimmering space shall I find what glimmering glory? The stark, stony mountainous surface is turned to green, rolling meadow, and a spring of clear water, its origins a mystery, its purpose and beauty constant, draws all manner of troubled existence seeking solace. And again and again, the heart—buried deeply as ever in the human breast, its four chambers exposed to love and joy and pain and the small shafts that fall with desperation in between.

~~

I sat at a narrow table, my head, heavy with sleep, resting on my hands. I dreamed of bands of men who walked aimlessly, their guns and cannons slackened at their sides, the chambers emptied of bullets and shells. They had fought in a field from time to time and from time to time they grew tired of it. They walked up the path that led to my house and as they walked they passed between the sun and the earth; as they passed between the sun and the earth they blotted out the daylight and night fell immediately and permanently. No longer could I see the blooming trefoils, their overpowering perfume a constant giddy delight to me; no longer could I see the domesticated animals feeding in the pasture; no longer could I see the beasts, hunter and prey, leading a guarded existence; no longer could I see the smith moving cautiously in a swirl of hot sparks or bent over anvil and bellows. The bands of men marched through my house in silence. On their way, their breath scorched some flowers I had placed on a dresser, with their bare hands they destroyed the marble columns that strengthened the foundations of my house. They left my house, in silence again, and they walked across a field, opposite to the way they had come, still passing between the sun and the earth. I stood at a window and watched their backs until they were just a small spot on the horizon.

~

I see my child arise slowly from her bed. I see her cross the room and stand in front of the mirror. She looks closely at her straight, unmarred body. Her skin is without color, and when passing through a small beam of light, she is made transparent. Her eyes are ruby, revolving orbs, and they burn like coals caught suddenly in a gust of wind. This is my child! When her jaws were too weak, I first chewed her food, then fed it to her in small mouthfuls. This is my child! I must carry a cool liquid in my flattened breasts to quench her parched throat. This is my child sitting in the shade, her head thrown back in rapture, prolonging some moment of joy I have created for her.

My child is pitiless to the hunchback boy; her mouth twists open in a cruel smile, her teeth becoming pointed and sparkling, the roof of her mouth bony and ridged, her young hands suddenly withered and gnarled as she reaches out to caress his hump. Squirming away from her forceful, heated gaze, he seeks shelter in a grove of trees, but her arms, which she can command to grow to incredible lengths, seek him out and tug at the long silk-like hairs that lie flattened on his back. She calls his name softly and the sound of her voice shatters his eardrum. Deaf, he can no longer heed warnings of danger and his sense of direction is destroyed. Still, my child has built for him a dwelling hut on the edge of a steep cliff so that she may watch him day after day flatten himself against a fate of which he knows and yet cannot truly know until the moment it consumes him.

My child haunts the dwelling places of the useless-

winged cormorants, so enamored is she of great
beauty and ancestral history. She traces each thing
from its meager happenstance beginnings in cool and
slimy marsh, to its great glory and dominance of air
or land or sea, to its odd remains entombed in mysterious alluviums. She loves the thing untouched by
lore, she loves the thing that is not cultivated, and
yet she loves the thing built up, bit carefully placed
upon bit, its very beauty eclipsing the deed it is meant
to commemorate. She sits idly on a shore, staring
hard at the sea beneath the sea and at the sea
beneath even that. She hears the sounds within the
sounds, common as that is to open spaces. She feels
the specter, first cold, then briefly warm, then cold
again as it passes from atmosphere to atmosphere.
Having observed the many differing physical exist-
ences feed on each other, she is beyond despair or
the spiritual vacuum.

Oh, look at my child as she stands boldly now, one
foot in the dark, the other in the light. Moving from
pool to pool, she absorbs each special sensation for
and of itself. My child rushes from death to death,
so familiar a state is it to her. Though I have sum-
moned her into a fleeting existence, one that is peril-
ous and subject to the violence of chance, she
embraces time as it passes in numbing sameness,
bearing in its wake a multitude of great sadnesses.

❧

I hear the silent voice; it stands opposite the blackness and yet it does not oppose the blackness, for conflict is not a part of its nature. I shrug off my mantle of hatred. In love I move toward the silent voice. I shrug off my mantle of despair. In love, again, I move ever toward the silent voice. I stand inside the silent voice. The silent voice enfolds me. The silent voice enfolds me so completely that even in memory the blackness is erased. I live in silence. The silence is without boundaries. The pastures are unfenced, the lions roam the continents, the continents are not separated. Across the flat lands cuts the river, its flow undammed. The mountains no longer rupture. Within the silent voice, no mysterious depths separate me; no vision is so distant that longing is stirred up in me. I hear the silent voice—how softly now it falls, and all of existence is caught up in it. Living in the silent voice, I am no longer "I." Living in the silent voice, I am at last at peace. Living in the silent voice, I am at last erased.

MY MOTHER

Immediately on wishing my mother dead and seeing the pain it caused her, I was sorry and cried so many tears that all the earth around me was drenched. Standing before my mother, I begged her forgiveness, and I begged so earnestly that she took pity on me, kissing my face and placing my head on her bosom to rest. Placing her arms around me, she drew my head closer and closer to her bosom, until finally I suffocated. I lay on her bosom, breathless, for a time uncountable, until one day, for a reason she has kept to herself, she shook me out and stood me under a tree and I started to breathe again. I cast a sharp glance at her and said to myself, "So." Instantly I grew my own bosoms, small mounds at first, leaving a small, soft place between them, where, if ever necessary, I could rest my own head. Between my mother and me now were the tears I had cried, and I gathered up some stones and banked them in so that they formed a small pond. The water in the pond was thick and black and poisonous, so that only unnamable invertebrates could live in it. My mother and I now watched each other carefully, always making sure to shower the other with words and deeds of love and affection.

I was sitting on my mother's bed trying to get a good look at myself. It was a large bed and it stood in the middle of a large, completely dark room. The room was completely dark because all the windows had been boarded up and all the crevices stuffed with black cloth. My mother lit some candles and the room burst into a pink-like, yellow-like glow. Looming over us, much larger than ourselves, were our shadows. We sat mesmerized because our shadows had made a place between themselves, as if they were making room for someone else. Nothing filled up the space between them, and the shadow of my mother sighed. The shadow of my mother danced around the room to a tune that my own shadow sang, and then they stopped. All along, our shadows had grown thick and thin, long and short, had fallen at every angle, as if they were controlled by the light of day. Suddenly my mother got up and blew out the candles and our shadows vanished. I continued to sit on the bed, trying to get a good look at myself.

❧

My mother removed her clothes and covered thoroughly her skin with a thick gold-colored oil, which had recently been rendered in a hot pan from the livers of reptiles with pouched throats. She grew plates of metal-colored scales on her back, and light, when it collided with this surface, would shatter and collapse into tiny points. Her teeth now arranged themselves into rows that reached all the way back to her long white throat. She uncoiled her hair from her head and then removed her hair altogether. Taking her head into her large palms, she flattened it so that her eyes, which were by now ablaze, sat on top of her head and spun like two revolving balls. Then, making two lines on the soles of each foot, she divided her feet into crossroads. Silently, she had instructed me to follow her example, and now I too traveled along on my white underbelly, my tongue darting and flickering in the hot air. "Look," said my mother.

❧

My mother and I were standing on the seabed side by side, my arms laced loosely around her waist, my head resting securely on her shoulder, as if I needed the support. To make sure she believed in my frail-

ness, I sighed occasionally—long soft sighs, the kind
of sigh she had long ago taught me could evoke
sympathy. In fact, how I really felt was invincible.
I was no longer a child but I was not yet a woman.
My skin had just blackened and cracked and fallen
away and my new impregnable carapace had taken
full hold. My nose had flattened; my hair curled in
and stood out straight from my head simultaneously;
my many rows of teeth in their retractable trays
were in place. My mother and I wordlessly made an
arrangement—I sent out my beautiful sighs, she re-
ceived them; I leaned ever more heavily on her for
support, she offered her shoulder, which shortly grew
to the size of a thick plank. A long time passed, at
the end of which I had hoped to see my mother
permanently cemented to the seabed. My mother
reached out to pass a hand over my head, a pacifying
gesture, but I laughed and, with great agility,
stepped aside. I let out a horrible roar, then a self-
pitying whine. I had grown big, but my mother was
bigger, and that would always be so. We walked to
the Garden of Fruits and there ate to our hearts'
satisfaction. We departed through the southwesterly
gate, leaving as always, in our trail, small colonies of
worms.

❦

With my mother, I crossed, unwillingly, the valley.
We saw a lamb grazing and when it heard our foot-

steps it paused and looked up at us. The lamb looked
cross and miserable. I said to my mother, "The lamb
is cross and miserable. So would I be, too, if I had
to live in a climate not suited to my nature." My
mother and I now entered the cave. It was the dark
and cold cave. I felt something growing under my
feet and I bent down to eat it. I stayed that way for
years, bent over eating whatever I found growing
under my feet. Eventually, I grew a special lens that
would allow me to see in the darkest of darkness;
eventually, I grew a special coat that kept me warm
in the coldest of coldness. One day I saw my mother
sitting on a rock. She said, "What a strange expres-
sion you have on your face. So cross, so miserable,
as if you were living in a climate not suited to your
nature." Laughing, she vanished. I dug a deep, deep
hole. I built a beautiful house, a floorless house, over
the deep, deep hole. I put in lattice windows, most
favored of windows by my mother, so perfect for
looking out at people passing by without her being observed. I painted the house itself yellow, the windows
green, colors I knew would please her. Standing just
outside the door, I asked her to inspect the house.
I said, "Take a look. Tell me if it's to your satisfaction." Laughing out of the corner of a mouth
I could not see, she stepped inside. I stood just outside the door, listening carefully, hoping to hear her
land with a thud at the bottom of the deep, deep

hole. Instead, she walked up and down in every direction, even pounding her heel on the air. Coming outside to greet me, she said, "It is an excellent house. I would be honored to live in it," and then vanished. I filled up the hole and burnt the house to the ground.

My mother has grown to an enormous height. I have grown to an enormous height also, but my mother's height is three times mine. Sometimes I cannot see from her breasts on up, so lost is she in the atmosphere. One day, seeing her sitting on the seashore, her hand reaching out in the deep to caress the belly of a striped fish as he swam through a place where two seas met, I glowed red with anger. For a while then I lived alone on the island where there were eight full moons and I adorned the face of each moon with expressions I had seen on my mother's face. All the expressions favored me. I soon grew tired of living in this way and returned to my mother's side. I remained, though glowing red with anger, and my mother and I built houses on opposite banks of the dead pond. The dead pond lay between us; in it, only small invertebrates with poisonous lances lived. My mother behaved toward them as if she had suddenly found herself in the same room with relatives we had long since risen above. I cherished their presence and gave them names. Still

I missed my mother's close company and cried constantly for her, but at the end of each day when I saw her return to her house, incredible and great deeds in her wake, each of them singing loudly her praises, I glowed and glowed again, red with anger. Eventually, I wore myself out and sank into a deep, deep sleep, the only dreamless sleep I have ever had.

❦

One day my mother packed my things in a grip and, taking me by the hand, walked me to the jetty, placed me on board a boat, in care of the captain. My mother, while caressing my chin and cheeks, said some words of comfort to me because we had never been apart before. She kissed me on the forehead and turned and walked away. I cried so much my chest heaved up and down, my whole body shook at the sight of her back turned toward me, as if I had never seen her back turned toward me before. I started to make plans to get off the boat, but when I saw that the boat was encased in a large green bottle, as if it were about to decorate a mantelpiece, I fell asleep, until I reached my destination, the new island. When the boat stopped, I got off and I saw a woman with feet exactly like mine, especially around the arch of the instep. Even though the face was completely different from what I was used to, I recognized this woman as my mother. We greeted each other at first with great caution and politeness, but as we walked along, our steps became one, and as we talked, our voices became one voice, and we were in complete union in every other way. What peace came over me then, for I could not see where she left off and I began, or where I left off and she began.

My mother and I walk through the rooms of her house. Every crack in the floor holds a significant event: here, an apparently healthy young man suddenly dropped dead; here a young woman defied her father and, while riding her bicycle to the forbidden lovers' meeting place, fell down a precipice, remaining a cripple for the rest of a very long life. My mother and I find this a beautiful house. The rooms are large and empty, opening on to each other, waiting for people and things to fill them up. Our white muslin skirts billow up around our ankles, our hair hangs straight down our backs as our arms hang straight at our sides. I fit perfectly in the crook of my mother's arm, on the curve of her back, in the hollow of her stomach. We eat from the same bowl, drink from the same cup; when we sleep, our heads rest on the same pillow. As we walk through the rooms, we merge and separate, merge and separate; soon we shall enter the final stage of our evolution.

The fishermen are coming in from sea; their catch is bountiful, my mother has seen to that. As the

waves plop, plop against each other, the fishermen
are happy that the sea is calm. My mother points out
the fishermen to me, their contentment is a source
of my contentment. I am sitting in my mother's
enormous lap. Sometimes I sit on a mat she has made
for me from her hair. The lime trees are weighed
down with limes—I have already perfumed myself
with their blossoms. A hummingbird has nested on
my stomach, a sign of my fertileness. My mother and
I live in a bower made from flowers whose petals are
imperishable. There is the silvery blue of the sea,
crisscrossed with sharp darts of light, there is the
warm rain falling on the clumps of castor bush, there
is the small lamb bounding across the pasture, there
is the soft ground welcoming the soles of my pink
feet. It is in this way my mother and I have lived
for a long time now.

AT THE BOTTOM

OF THE RIVER

This, then, is the terrain. The steepest mountains, thickly covered, where huge, sharp
rocks might pose the greatest danger and where only
the bravest, surest, most deeply arched of human
feet will venture, where a large stream might flow,
and, flowing perilously, having only a deep ambition
to see itself mighty and powerful, bends and curves
and dips in many directions, making a welcome and
easy path for each idle rill and babbling brook, each
trickle of rain fallen on land that lies sloping; and
that stream, at last swelled to a great, fast, flowing
body of water, falls over a ledge with a roar, a loud-
ness that is more than the opposite of complete
silence, then rushes over dry, flat land in imperfect
curves—curves as if made by a small boy playfully
dragging a toy behind him—then hugs closely to the

paths made, ruthlessly conquering the flat plain, the steep ridge, the grassy bed; all day, all day, a stream might flow so, and then it winds its way to a gorge in the earth, a basin of measurable depth and breadth, and so collects itself in a pool: now comes the gloaming, for day will end, and the stream, its flow stilled and gathered up, so that trees growing firmly on its banks, their barks white, their trunks bent, their branches covered with leaves and reaching up, up, are reflected in the depths, awaits the eye, the hand, the foot that shall then give all this a meaning.

But what shall that be? For now here is a man who lives in a world bereft of its very nature. He lies on his bed as if alone in a small room, waiting and waiting and waiting. For what does he wait? He is not yet complete, so he cannot conceive of what it is he waits for. He cannot conceive of the fields of wheat, their kernels ripe and almost bursting, and how happy the sight will make someone. He cannot conceive of the union of opposites, or, for that matter, their very existence. He cannot conceive of flocks of birds in migratory flight, or that night will follow day and season follow season in a seemingly endless cycle, and the beauty and the pleasure and the purpose that might come from all this. He cannot conceive of the wind that ravages the coastline, casting asunder men and cargo, temporarily interrupting the smooth flow of commerce. He cannot conceive of the individual who, on looking up from some dreary, everyday task, is struck just then by the completeness of the above and the below and his own spirit resting in between; or how that same individual, suddenly rounding a corner, catches his own reflection, transparent and suspended in a pane of glass, and so smiles to himself with shy admiration. He cannot conceive of the woman and the child at play—an image so often regarded as a symbol of human contentment; or how calamity will attract the cold and disinterested gaze of children. He cannot conceive of a Sunday: the peal of church bells, the sound of seraphic voices in harmony, the closeness of congregation, the soothing words of praise and the much longed for presence of an unearthly glory. He cannot conceive of how emotions, varying in color and intensity, will rapidly heighten, reach an unbearable pitch, then finally explode in the silence of the evening air. He cannot conceive of the chance invention that changes again and again and forever the great turbulence that is human history. Not for him can thought crash over thought in random and violent succession, leaving his brain suffused in contradiction. He sits in nothing, this man: not in a full space, not in emptiness, not in darkness, not in light or glimmer of. He sits in nothing, in nothing, in nothing.

≈❤

Look! A man steps out of bed, a good half hour
after his wife, and washes himself. He sits down on
a chair and at a table that he made with his own
hands (the tips of his fingers are stained a thin choco-
late brown from nicotine). His wife places before
him a bowl of porridge, some cheese, some bread that
has been buttered, two boiled eggs, a large cup of
tea. He eats. The goats, the sheep, the cows are
driven to pasture. A dog barks. His child now enters
the room. Walking over, she bends to kiss his hand,
which is resting on his knee, and he, waiting for her
head to come up, kisses her on the forehead with lips
he has purposely moistened. "Sir, it is wet," she says.
And he laughs at her as she dries her forehead with
the back of her hand. Now, clasping his wife to him,
he bids her goodbye, opens the door, and stops. For
what does he stop? What does he see? He sees
before him himself, standing in sawdust, measuring
a hole, just dug, in the ground, putting decorative
grooves in a bannister, erecting columns, carving the
head of a cherub over a door, lighting a cigarette,
pursing his lips, holding newly planed wood at an
angle and looking at it with one eye closed; standing
with both hands in his pockets, the thumbs out, and
rocking back and forth on his heels, he surveys a
small accomplishment—a last nail driven in just so.
Crossing and recrossing the threshold, he watches
the sun, a violent red, set on the horizon, he hears

the birds fly home, he sees the insects dancing in the
last warmth of the day's light, he hears himself sing
out loud:

> *Now the day is over,*
> *Night is drawing nigh;*
> *Shadows of the evening*
> *Steal across the sky.*

All this he sees (and hears). And who is this man,
really? So solitary, his eyes sometimes aglow, his
heart beating at an abnormal rate with a joy he cannot identify or explain. What is the virtue in him?
And then again, what can it matter? For tomorrow
the oak will be felled, the trestle will break, the
cow's hooves will be made into glue.

But so he stands, forever, crossing and recrossing
the threshold, his head lifted up, held aloft and stiff
with vanity; then his eyes shift and he sees and he
sees, and he is weighed down. First lifted up, then
weighed down—always he is so. Shall he seek comfort now? And in what? He seeks out the living
fossils. There is the shell of the pearly nautilus lying
amidst colored chalk and powdered ink and India
rubber in an old tin can, in memory of a day spent
blissfully at the sea. The flatworm is now a para-
site. Reflect. There is the earth, its surface apparently stilled, its atmosphere hospitable. And yet here
stand pile upon pile of rocks of an enormous size,

riven and worn down from the pressure of the great seas, now receded. And here the large veins of gold, the bubbling sulfurous fountains, the mountains covered with hot lava; at the bottom of some caves lies the black dust, and below that rich clay sediment, and trapped between the layers are filaments of winged beasts and remnants of invertebrates. "And where shall I be?" asks this man. Then he says, "My body, my soul." But quickly he averts his eyes and feels himself now, hands pressed tightly against his chest. He is standing on the threshold once again, and, looking up, he sees his wife holding out toward him his brown felt hat (he had forgotten it); his child crossing the street, joining the throng of children on their way to school, a mixture of broken sentences, mispronounced words, laughter, budding malice, and energy abundant. He looks at the house he has built with his own hands, the books he has read standing on shelves, the fruit-bearing trees that he nursed from seedlings, the larder filled with food that he has provided. He shifts the weight of his body from one foot to the other, in uncertainty but also weighing, weighing . . . He imagines that in one hand he holds emptiness and yearning and in the other desire fulfilled. He thinks of tenderness and love and faith and hope and, yes, goodness. He contemplates the beauty in the common thing: the sun rising up out of the huge, shimmering expanse of water that is the sea; it rises up each day as if made anew, as if for the first time. "Sing again. Sing now," he says in his heart, for he feels the cool breeze at the back of his neck. But again and again he feels the futility in all that. For stretching out before him is a silence so dreadful, a vastness, its length and breadth and depth immeasurable. Nothing.

❧

The branches were dead; a fly hung dead on the branches, its fragile body fluttering in the wind as if it were remnants of a beautiful gown; a beetle had fed on the body of the fly but now lay dead, too. Death on death on death. Dead lay everything. The ground stretching out from the river no longer a verdant pasture but parched and cracked with tiny fissures running up and down and into each other; and, seen from high above, the fissures presented beauty: not a pleasure to the eye but beauty all the same; still, dead, dead it was. Dead lay everything that had lived and dead also lay everything that would live. All had had or would have its season. And what should it matter that its season lasted five billion years or five minutes? There it is now, dead, vanished into darkness, banished from life. First living briefly, then dead in eternity. How vainly I struggle against this. Toil, toil, night and day. Here a house is built. Here a monument is erected to commemorate something called a good deed, or even in remembrance of a woman with exceptional qualities, and all that she loved and all that she did. Here are some children, and immeasurable is the love and special attention lavished on them. Vanished now is the house. Vanished now is the monument. Silent now are the children. I recall the house, I recall the monument, I summon up the children from the eternity of darkness, and sometimes, briefly, they appear, though always slightly shrouded, always as if they had emerged from mounds of ashes, chipped, tarnished, in fragments, or large parts missing: the ribbons, for instance, gone from the children's hair. These children whom I loved best—better than the monument, better than the house—once were so beautiful that they were thought unearthly. Dead is the past. Dead shall the future be. And what stands before my eyes, as soon as I turn my back, dead is that, too. Shall I shed tears? Sorrow is bound to death. Grief is bound to death. Each moment is not as fragile and fleeting as I once thought. Each moment is hard and lasting and so holds much that I must mourn for. And so what a bitter thing to say to me: that life is the intrusion, that to embrace a thing as beauty is the intrusion, that to believe a thing true and therefore undeniable, that is the intrusion; and, yes, false are all appearances. What a bitter thing to say to me, I who for time uncountable have always seen myself as newly born, filled with a

truth and a beauty that could not be denied, living
in a world of light that I called eternal, a world that
can know no end. I now know regret. And that, too,
is bound to death. And what do I regret? Surely not
that I stand in the knowledge of the presence of
death. For knowledge is a good thing; you have said
that. What I regret is that in the face of death and
all that it is and all that it shall be I stand powerless,
that in the face of death my will, to which everything
I have ever known bends, stands as if it were nothing
more than a string caught in the early-morning wind.

Now! There lived a small creature, and it lived
as both male and female inside a mound that it made
on the ground, its body wholly covered with short
fur, broadly striped, in the colors field-yellow and
field-blue. It hunted a honeybee once, and when the
bee, in bee anger and fright, stung the creature on
the corner of the mouth, the pain was so unbearably
delicious that never did this creature hunt a honeybee
again. It walked over and over the wide space that
surrounded the mound in which it lived. As it walked
over and over the wide ground that surrounded the
mound in which it lived, it watched its own feet sink
into the grass and heard the ever so slight sound
the grass made as it gave way to the pressure, and as
it saw and heard, it felt a pleasure unbearably
delicious, and, each time, the pleasure unbearably
delicious was new to this creature. It lived so, bank-

ing up each unbearably delicious pleasure in deep,
dark memory unspeakable, hoping to perhaps one
day throw the memories into a dungeon, or burn
them on an ancient pyre, or banish them to land
barren, but now it kept them in this way. Then all its
unbearably delicious pleasure it kept free, each thing
taken, time in, time out, as if it were new, just born.
It lived so in a length of time that may be measured
to be no less than the blink of an eye, or no more
than one hundred millenniums. This creature lived
inside and outside its mound, remembering and
forgetting, pain and pleasure so equally balanced,
each assigned to what it judged a natural conclusion,
yet one day it did vanish, leaving no sign of its existence, except for a small spot, which glowed faintly
in the darkness that surrounded it. I divined this, and
how natural to me that has become. I divined this,
and it is not a specter but something that stood here.
I show it to you. I yearn to build a monument to it,
something of dust, since I now know—and so soon,
so soon—what dust really is.

"Death is natural," you said to me, in such a flat,
matter-of-fact way, and then you laughed—a laugh
so piercing that I felt my eardrums shred, I felt
myself mocked. Yet I can see that a tree is natural,
that the sea is natural, that the twitter of a twittering
bird is natural to a twittering bird. I can see with my
own eyes the tree; it stands with limbs spread wide

and laden with ripe fruit, its roots planted firmly in
the rich soil, and that seems natural to me. I can
see with my own eyes the sea, now with a neap tide,
its surface smooth and calm; then in the next moment
comes a breeze, soft, and small ripples turn into
wavelets conquering wavelets, and that seems natural
to me again. And the twittering bird twitters away,
and that bears a special irritation, though not the
irritation of the sting of the evening fly, and that
special irritation is mostly ignored, and what could
be more natural than that? But death bears no rela-
tion to the tree, the sea, the twittering bird. How
much more like the earth spinning on its invisible axis
death is, and so I might want to reach out with my
hand and make the earth stand still, as if it were a
bicycle standing on its handlebars upside down, the
wheels spun in passing by a pair of idle hands, then
stilled in passing by yet another pair of idle hands.
Inevitable to life is death and not inevitable to death
is life. Inevitable. How the word weighs on my
tongue. I glean this: a worm winds its way between
furrow and furrow in a garden, its miserable form
shuddering, dreading the sharp open beak of any
common bird winging its way overhead; the bird,
then taking to the open air, spreads its wings in
majestic flight, and how noble and triumphant is this
bird in flight; but look now, there comes a boy on
horseback, his body taut and eager, his hand holding

bow and arrow, his aim pointed and definite, and in this way is the bird made dead. The worm, the bird, the boy. And what of the boy? His ends are number-less. I glean again the death in life.

❦

Is life, then, a violent burst of light, like flint struck sharply in the dark? If so, I must continually strive to exist between the day and the day. I see myself as I was as a child. How much I was loved and how much I loved. No small turn of my head, no wrinkle on my brow, no parting of my lips is lost to me. How much I loved myself and how much I was loved by my mother. My mother made up elaborate tales of the origins of ordinary food, just so that I would eat it. My mother sat on some stone steps, her volumi-nous skirt draped in folds and falling down between her parted legs, and I, playing some distance away, glanced over my shoulder and saw her face—a face that was to me of such wondrous beauty: the lips like a moon in its first and last quarter, a nose with a bony bridge and wide nostrils that flared out and trembled visibly in excitement, ears the lobes of which were large and soft and silk-like; and what pleasure it gave me to press them between my thumb and forefinger. How I worshipped this beauty, and in my childish heart I would always say to it, "Yes, yes, yes." And, glancing over my shoulder, yet again I would silently send to her words of love and adoration, and I would receive from her, in turn and in silence, words of love and adoration. Once, I stood on a platform with three dozen girls, arranged in rows of twelve, all wearing identical white linen dresses with corded sashes of green tied around the waist, all with faces the color of stones found lying on the beach of volcanic islands, singing with the utmost earnestness, in as nearly perfect a harmony as could be managed, minds blank of interpretation:

> *In our deep vaulted cell*
> *The charm we'll prepare*
> *Too dreadful a practice*
> *For this open air.*

Time and time again, I am filled up with all that I thought life might be—glorious moment upon glorious moment of contentment and joy and love running into each other and forming an extraordinary chain: a hymn sung in rounds. Oh, the fields in which I have walked and gazed and gazed at the small cuplike flowers, in wanton hues of red and gold and blue, swaying in the day breeze, and from which I had no trouble tearing myself away, since their end was unknown to me.

☙

I walked to the mouth of the river, and it was then still in the old place near the lime-tree grove. The water was clear and still. I looked in, and at the bottom of the river I could see a house, and it was a house of only one room, with an A-shaped roof. The house was made of rough, heavy planks of unpainted wood, and the roof was of galvanized iron and was painted red. The house had four windows on each of its four sides, and one door. Though the door and the windows were all open, I could not see anything inside and I had no desire to see what was inside. All around the house was a wide stretch of green—green grass freshly mowed a uniform length. The green, green grass of uniform length extended from the house for a distance I could not measure or know just from looking at it. Beyond the green, green grass were lots of pebbles, and they were a white-gray, as if they had been in water for many years and then placed in the sun to dry. They, too, were of a uniform size, and as they lay together they seemed to form a direct contrast to the grass. Then, at the line where the grass ended and the pebbles began, there were flowers: yellow and blue irises, red poppies, daffodils, marigolds. They grew as if wild, intertwined, as if no hand had ever offered guidance or restraint. There were no other living things in the water—no birds, no vertebrates or inverte-brates, no fragile insects—and even though the water flowed in the natural way of a river, none of the things that I could see at the bottom moved. The grass, in little wisps, didn't bend slightly; the petals of the flowers didn't tremble. Everything was so true, though—that is, true to itself—and I had no doubt that the things I saw were themselves and not resemblances or representatives. The grass was the grass, and it was the grass without qualification. The green of the grass was green, and I knew it to be so and not partially green, or a kind of green, but green, and the green from which all other greens might come. And it was so with everything else that lay so still at the bottom of the river. It all lay there not like a picture but like a true thing and a different kind of true thing: one that I had never known before. Then I noticed something new: it was the way everything lit up. It was as if the sun shone not from where I stood but from a place way beyond and beneath the ground of the grass and the pebbles. How strange the light was, how it filled up everything, and yet nothing cast a shadow. I looked and looked at what was before me in wonderment and curiosity. What should this mean to me? And what should I do on knowing its meaning? A woman now appeared at the one door. She wore no clothes. Her hair was long and so very black, and it stood out in a straight line away from her head, as if she had commanded it to be that way. I could not see her face. I could see her feet, and I saw that her insteps were high, as if she had been used to climbing high mountains. Her skin was the color of brown clay, and she

looked like a statue, liquid and gleaming, just before
it is to be put in a kiln. She walked toward the place
where the grass ended and the pebbles began. Perhaps it was a great distance, it took such a long time,
and yet she never tired. When she got to the place
where the green grass ended and the pebbles began,
she stopped, then raised her right hand to her forehead, as if to guard her eyes against a far-off glare.
She stood on tiptoe, her body swaying from side
to side, and she looked at something that was far,
far away from where she stood. I got down on my
knees and I looked, too. It was a long time before
I could see what it was that she saw.

I saw a world in which the sun and the moon shone
at the same time. They appeared in a way I had
never seen before: the sun was The Sun, a creation
of Benevolence and Purpose and not a star among
many stars, with a predictable cycle and a predictable
end; the moon, too, was The Moon, and it was the
creation of Beauty and Purpose and not a body
subject to a theory of planetary evolution. The sun
and the moon shone uniformly onto everything. Together, they made up the light, and the light fell on
everything, and everything seemed transparent, as if
the light went through each thing, so that nothing
could be hidden. The light shone and shone and fell
and fell, but there were no shadows. In this world,
on this terrain, there was no day and there was no

night. And there were no seasons, and so no storms
or cold from which to take shelter. And in this world
were many things blessed with unquestionable truth
and purpose and beauty. There were steep mountains, there were valleys, there were seas, there were
plains of grass, there were deserts, there were rivers,
there were forests, there were vertebrates and invertebrates, there were mammals, there were reptiles, there were creatures of the dry land and the
water, and there were birds. And they lived in this
world not yet divided, not yet examined, not yet
numbered, and not yet dead. I looked at this world
as it revealed itself to me—how new, how new—
and I longed to go there.

I stood above the land and the sea and looked back
up at myself as I stood on the bank of the mouth of
the river. I saw that my face was round in shape,
that my irises took up almost all the space in my eyes,
and that my eyes were brown, with yellow-colored
and black-colored flecks; that my mouth was large
and closed; that my nose, too, was large and my
nostrils broken circles; my arms were long, my hands
large, the veins pushing up against my skin; my legs
were long, and, judging from the shape of them, I
was used to running long distances. I saw that my
hair grew out long from my head and in a disorderly
way, as if I were a strange tree, with many branches.
I saw my skin, and it was red. It was the red of

flames when a fire is properly fed, the red of flames when a fire burns alone in a darkened place, and not the red of flames when a fire is burning in a cozy room. I saw myself clearly, as if I were looking through a pane of glass.

I stood above the land and the sea, and I felt that I was not myself as I had once known myself to be: I was not made up of flesh and blood and muscles and bones and tissue and cells and vital organs but was made up of my will, and over my will I had complete dominion. I entered the sea then. The sea was without color, and it was without anything that I had known before. It was still, having no currents. It was as warm as freshly spilled blood, and I moved through it as if I had always done so, as if it were a perfectly natural element to me. I moved through deep caverns, but they were without darkness and sudden shifts and turns. I stepped over great ridges and huge bulges of stones, I stooped down and touched the deepest bottom; I stretched myself out and covered end to end a vast crystal plane. Nothing lived here. No plant grew here, no huge sharp-toothed creature with an ancestral memory of hunter and prey searching furiously for food, no sudden shift of wind to disturb the water. How good this water was. How good that I should know no fear. I sat on the edge of a basin. I felt myself swing my feet back and forth in a carefree manner, as if I

were a child who had just spent the whole day head
bent over sums but now sat in a garden filled with
flowers in bloom colored vermillion and gold, the
sounds of birds chirping, goats bleating, home from
the pasture, the smell of vanilla from the kitchen,
which should surely mean pudding with dinner, eyes
darting here and there but resting on nothing in
particular, a mind conscious of nothing—not happi-
ness, not contentment, and not the memory of night,
which soon would come.

I stood up on the edge of the basin and felt myself
move. But what self? For I had no feet, or hands, or
head, or heart. It was as if those things—my feet,
my hands, my head, my heart—having once been
there, were now stripped away, as if I had been
dipped again and again, over and over, in a large vat
filled with some precious elements and were now reduced to something I yet had no name for. I had no
name for the thing I had become, so new was it to
me, except that I did not exist in pain or pleasure,
east or west or north or south, or up or down, or
past or present or future, or real or not real. I stood
as if I were a prism, many-sided and transparent,
refracting and reflecting light as it reached me, light
that never could be destroyed. And how beautiful I
became. Yet this beauty was not in the way of an
ancient city seen after many centuries in ruins, or a
woman who has just brushed her hair, or a man who

searches for a treasure, or a child who cries immediately on being born, or an apple just picked standing
alone on a gleaming white plate, or tiny beads of
water left over from a sudden downpour of rain,
perhaps—hanging delicately from the bare limbs of
trees—or the sound the hummingbird makes with
its wings as it propels itself through the earthly air.

～

Yet what was that light in which I stood? How
singly then will the heart desire and pursue the small
glowing thing resting in the distance, surrounded by
darkness; how, then, if on conquering the distance
the heart embraces the small glowing thing until
heart and glowing thing are indistinguishable and in
this way the darkness is made less? For now a door
might suddenly be pushed open and the morning light
might rush in, revealing to me creation and a force
whose nature is implacable, unmindful of any of the
individual needs of existence, and without knowledge
of future or past. I might then come to believe in a
being whose impartiality I cannot now or ever fully
understand and accept. I ask, When shall I, too, be
extinguished, so that I cannot be recognized even
from my bones? I covet the rocks and the mountains
their silence. And so, emerging from my pit, the one
I sealed up securely, the one to which I have con-
signed all my deeds that I care not to reveal—
emerging from this pit, I step into a room and I see

that the lamp is lit. In the light of the lamp, I see
some books, I see a chair, I see a table, I see a pen;
I see a bowl of ripe fruit, a bottle of milk, a flute
made of wood, the clothes that I will wear. And as
I see these things in the light of the lamp, all
perishable and transient, how bound up I know I
am to all that is human endeavor, to all that is past
and to all that shall be, to all that shall be lost and
leave no trace. I claim these things then—mine—
and now feel myself grow solid and complete, my
name filling up my mouth.

Jamaica Kincaid's

LUCY

is

"Cool and fierce . . . The toughness and elegance of Kincaid's writing is all that one could want."

—*Washington Post Book World*

"Beautifully precise prose . . . it leaves the reader with the unforgettable experience of having met a ferociously honest woman on her own uncompromising terms."

—*New York Times*

"Brilliant . . . *Lucy* confirms Ms. Kincaid as both a daughter of Brontë and Woolf and her own inimitable self."

—*Wall Street Journal*

"A furious, broken-hearted gem of a novel . . . part of the richness of this book is the way we come to see, as Lucy struggles to do, the connections between those who have too much and who will never have enough—and between 'a sentence for life' (what can't be changed in the self) and that which can be wrestled with and, at least, understood."

—*San Francisco Chronicle*

PLUME

Contemporary Fiction for Your Enjoyment

☐ **THE ARISTOS by John Fowles.** A wonderfully fascinating and original novel covering the whole range of human experience: good and evil, pleasure and pain, sex and socialism, Christianity and star-gazing. "A remarkable talent."—*New York Times*   (260442—$8.95)

☐ **MANTISSA by John Fowles.** The author of *The French Lieutenant's Woman* plays his most provocative game with art, eros, and the imagination . . . leading the reader through a labyrinth of romantic mystery and stunning revelation. "Tantalizing and entertaining!"—*Time*   (254299—$7.95)

☐ **MIDDLE PASSAGE by Charles Johnson.** "A story of slavery . . . a tale of travel and tragedy, yearning and history . . . brilliant, riveting."—*San Francisco Chronicle*   (266386—$8.95)

☐ **FAMOUS ALL OVER TOWN by Danny Santiago.** This is the Los Angeles of the Chicano barrio, where everything is stacked against the teenaged hero, Chato Medina, his beleaguered family, his defiant and doomed friends, and the future he may not make it far enough to enjoy. Chato, however, is out to beat all the odds—his own way . . .   (259746—$8.95)

Prices slightly higher in Canada.

Buy them at your local bookstore or use this convenient coupon for ordering.

NEW AMERICAN LIBRARY
P.O. Box 999, Bergenfield, New Jersey 07621

Please send me the books I have checked above.
I am enclosing $_____ (please add $2.00 to cover postage and handling).
Send check or money order (no cash or C.O.D.'s) or charge by Mastercard or VISA (with a $15.00 minimum). Prices and numbers are subject to change without notice.

Card # _____ Exp. Date _____

Signature _____

Name _____

Address _____

City _____ State _____ Zip Code _____

For faster service when ordering by credit card call 1-800-253-6476

Allow a minimum of 4-6 weeks for delivery. This offer is subject to change without notice

Four insightful novels from
PLUME AMERICAN WOMEN WRITERS...

☐ **ANGEL ISLAND by Inez Haynes Gilmore.** "A book of sound prosaic truths, as well as high ideals and beautiful imaginings."—*The New York Times.* Five bold men wash ashore on an island of glorious winged women. A remarkable work comparable to Charlotte Perkins Gilman's *Herland, Angel Island* never loses the excitement of a top-notch adventure story.   (262003—$8.95)

☐ **PINK AND WHITE TYRANNY by Harriet Beecher Stowe.** A charmingly entertaining—and astute—look at the institution of marriage by the ground-breaking author of *Uncle Tom's Cabin.* When the spoiled and petted Lillie tricks naive Mr. Seymour into marriage, it is unclear who is the victim and who the victimized. Ms. Stowe levels sharp criticism at a society that demands nothing of its women but charm and beauty.   (261775—$7.95)

☐ **EX-WIFE by Ursula Parrott.** Deemed as scandalous when it was first published in 1929, Ursula Parrott's bold and insightful novel is about the Jazz Age women known as "left-over ladies," trying to survive in a world run by men. Its penetrating glimpse of American women under or outside the pillars of marriage may seem strangely familiar to modern women.   (262240—$7.95)

☐ **BELOVED by Toni Morrison.** Winner of the 1988 Pulitzer Prize for Fiction. Sethe. Proud and beautiful, she escaped from slavery but is haunted by its heritage. Set in rural Ohio several years after the Civil War, this is a profoundly affecting chronicle and its aftermath. "A masterpiece . . . magnificent . . . astounding . . . overpowering!" —*Newsweek*   (264464—$9.95)

Prices slightly higher in Canada.

Buy them at your local bookstore or use this convenient coupon for ordering.

NEW AMERICAN LIBRARY
P.O. Box 999, Bergenfield, New Jersey 07621

Please send me the books I have checked above.
I am enclosing $_____ (please add $2.00 to cover postage and handling).
Send check or money order (no cash or C.O.D.'s) or charge by Mastercard or VISA (with a $15.00 minimum). Prices and numbers are subject to change without notice.

Card # _____ Exp. Date _____

Signature _____

Name _____

Address _____

City _____ State _____ Zip Code _____

For faster service when ordering by credit card call 1-800-253-6476

Allow a minimum of 4-6 weeks for delivery. This offer is subject to change without notice